My
Father's
Hands
MICHAEL

AF430784

My Father's Hands

Michael Lynes

Published by Michael Lynes, 2018.

While every precaution has been taken in the preparation of this book, the publisher assumes no responsibility for errors or omissions, or for damages resulting from the use of the information contained herein.

MY FATHER'S HANDS

First edition. February 17, 2018.

Copyright © 2018 Michael Lynes.

ISBN: 979-8602753691

Written by Michael Lynes.

Table of Contents

To my Father...thank you Dad.

MY FATHER'S HANDS

HANDS FASCINATE ME: maker's hands,
builder's hands, hands that mow the lawn, wash the car, or cook a great meal. Engineer's hands, conduits through which thoughts become deeds both great and small. Splayed thumb and calloused fingers, broad and scarred with work and play. Competent hands.

Hands tell our story. Each day they feed, lift, caress and guide, hold, and shape. My hands, once soft and small, youthful and passionate, now bear rings and cares and the lines of age. I am struck by how well I know them, how familiar they are. They are my hands, but they belonged first to another.

I look up from them and upon him. Peaceful in repose, he is the tallest and strongest man in the world. His eyes are veiled, but I know they are bright and blue and clear as a morning in Kerry. His broad chest rises and falls with each rhythmic, assisted breath. His hand rests upon it, pale and still.

He stirs.

I know I shouldn't hope, but I hope anyway. My eyes are drawn, unwilling, past the blinking pumps, past the coiled nest of tubes, to the displays above his head. I know what I will see there, but I want to disbelieve.

"He is indestructible," my heart whispers, "stronger than any man I have ever known. Nothing can harm him. No burden is too heavy, no problem beyond the skill of his hands. . .my hands. . . ."

I look down at them, useless counterfeits, powerless to do what must be done.

"He would not want to live this way, his soul imprisoned in his own flesh, his voice forever stilled, his very breath forced upon him." I shake my head in disbelief and sorrow.

Only ten days ago, some now-forgotten project had me busy in my lab, and I'd worked through the noon break as usual. Starving, I'd taken one bite out of my brown bag lunch when the extension rang. "Engineering," I said as I picked up the receiver, consciously copying the way Dad always answered the phone at his lab. On the other end of the line there was silence for a long moment. Then I heard my mother's voice, so low as to be almost a whisper. "I found Daddy collapsed on the floor," she said, each hoarse word filled with pain. "We're at the emergency room now. . . . They—they don't know what's wrong. . . ."

I could not speak. A wave of icy cold rolled through me. I could feel the blood drain from my face and hands. My heart leapt into my throat, and a staccato drumbeat began to pound in my ears. Sudden terror engulfed me like a choking cloud. My nerveless hands clenched around the receiver, pressing it to my ear. Frozen in that split instant of shock, somehow, his words came to me.

Be brave, I heard him say. You have to be brave. Your mother needs you, now more than ever before.

I swallowed hard, drew a deep breath, and found my own voice. "Mom," I said, his words allowing me to marshal my fear, "I'm on my way."

That night he was admitted for emergency neurosurgery, a ruptured artery in his brain. All of us, my sisters, and brother, and I, stood vigil with our mother for hours in the waiting room, but when the surgeon emerged, his news was guarded. "Your husband has suffered a massive inter-cranial bleed," he said to my mother, his words at once compassionate and chilling. "I have repaired the damaged vessel, and I've drained as much of the blood as possible." He paused for a beat, allowing us all to absorb the information. "The next week to ten days will be critical for his prognosis. The bleed was very extensive, and the severity of the damage is difficult to assess."

Mother's face was ashen, but she was calm. We gathered round her and listened as he continued, "We will know more once he comes out of sedation. For now, there is nothing more that can be done."

She thanked him, and a silent tear formed and began to flow down her cheek. I realized she had been holding my hand since the surgeon started speaking.

———— ❦ ————

YESTERDAY. WE GATHERED as before, hope and dread alike in our hearts. Clear and calm, the words of the surgeon cut into us like blades of ice cold steel: "Brain death."

His declaration washes over us all, cleaving an invisible wound, bloodless yet mortal. He continues, explaining the results of the many scans, the irreparable nature of damaged brain tissue, the impossibility of prolonged survival, the finality.

I am present. . .but I have stopped listening. My spirit is overcome. I think of all that my father is and was to me, to us all—his laughter, his strength, his bright eyes, skill of hand and thought and deed, all this, the making of a man, gone. His soul, that immortal, indestructible spark, is surely whole. His body, the flawed temple to which it remains bound, is broken. Our hope in medicine, in man, in the God-given gift of miraculous healing, is no more. His body is damaged unto death, yet it is so strong that it will not die.

". . .We can keep him on life support for now. His condition is critical but stable." The surgeon pauses for a long moment. "If you have any ques—"

"Doctor—" it is my voice rising unbidden, words forming almost without my volition— "are you sure? Is there any chance, with time. . . ?"

He looks at me, at all of us gathered round the bedside, and his reply is soft but firm. "No. The tissue damage and swelling is too severe. Your father's heart is still strong, but he cannot breathe without assistance, and the scans show no brain activity." He pauses for another long moment. "I-I'm sorry, but he is gone. Only his body lives on."

⸻ ❧ ⸻

8

TODAY, THE LAST DAY, each of us has taken some time to be alone with him, to say our farewells.

You would have known, I plead. *You would be able to make your hands obey. I am lost.*

God, why? Why did you give me his hands? I am not worthy of them. He taught me to be strong, to never give up, to believe. I bow my head once more, seeking solace, sanction, forgiveness, absolution.

"Help me, Father," I pray, "help me, God, to let your will be done. Help me. *Deus meus. Ex toto corde poenitet me omnium meorum peccatorum.* My confession is sincere, Father. My sins are blackest stain. I do not deserve your grace, your peace." A burning tear escapes; reproach, bitter and salt, wets my lips. Soundless I scream, *I spent my whole life! My whole life, trying to be like you! I am not worthy of you, of your hands. I am not ready. I will never be.*

Tears flow hot, unchecked, and I hide my face in shame, in anger at my weakness. Exhausted, I kneel on the sterile floor and rest my head next to his. The hospital linens are alien, soft, smelling faintly antiseptic. I don't care. I can feel the warmth of his body, the rhythm of his steady beating heart. I place my full hand beneath his empty one. My eyes close.

IT WAS OUR LAST FULL DAY of vacation.

Tomorrow we would be packing up, cleaning out, and piling into our big white station wagon for the long, hot trip home. Our late August week at the seashore had flown by. I wanted to squeeze as much fun as possible into the remaining hours.

Dumping my load of gear down next to our half set-up umbrella and towels, I ran over the hard-packed sand and threw myself into the water, my younger sister and brother not far behind. "Stay close!" Mom cautioned. "You have to wait for Dad before you go out. . .the water looks rough today."

"Aw," we chorused together. "I wanna go out deep!" I added. I'd spent the week learning to body-surf the breakers into the shallows, and my eight-year-old ego wanted to show off.

"Your father will be here in a minute. Just wait!"

Mom had her stern face on, so we contented ourselves with knee-deep play. It was not long before Dad appeared over the dune, his strong hands carrying my youngest sister and the rest of our seaside encampment. I always marveled how he could carry so many things. We ran back to the towels to "help" and dance around him, begging to go to the water.

"Okay, guys. . .okay!" That steady baritone brought us to attention. "Now, take my hand, and stay close." He extended a long forefinger to my brother, hoisted my youngest sister, her blond tresses blowing in the sea-breeze, up onto his broad shoulder, and set off down to the surf, my other sister and I trailing behind. The sun was bright and late August hot, and with Dad standing tall beside us all, it was going to be a great beach day.

I WAS OUT TOO FAR. Chin-high in the choppy wash, I could feel my toes dragging as each wave crest passed me by. The storm the night before had churned up the surf, and the sand below was loose, with patches of seaweed and stone and broken shells. I was the oldest, and I was proud that Dad would let me go out in the waves on my own. He trusted me to stay close to shore while he was watching my younger sibs, especially my baby sister. I thought I was a pretty strong swimmer, but the ocean was more powerful than I knew.

Saltwater filled my mouth. I choked and sputtered. The last wave broke just past my head, and the slap of cold spray half blinded me. I twisted around, doggy-paddling to keep my head above the foam, and caught sight of Dad. He was farther down the beach, holding my baby sister, both hands helping her jump each tiny leftover wave crest.

I could feel the wave start to pull back, dragging me with it. My toes lost contact with the sand, and then I was bobbing for air, unable to get enough to cry out.

"Dad," I croaked. "Help! I *need* you!" But I knew he could not hear me. My arms were getting tired, pulse pounding in my ears. I remembered him telling me to kick my legs. *Use your legs, and your feet, not your arms. If you get in trouble, kick!*

I spread my aching arms out and kicked my legs, willing my body to rise up. The waves were coming faster; the tide had turned, and the crests carried heads of angry froth. Arms outstretched, I kicked as hard as I could, trying to catch up with the swells as they rushed past me.

Eyes fixed upon the sand and safety, I forget to watch the breakers. My legs were burning by then, mouth half-submerged with each weakening thrust. A fleck of sea foam slipped down my throat, gagging me, cutting off my air. Sudden roaring filled my ears. Water, dark and green and boiling with foam, closed over my head. I felt myself tumbling, thrashing in a sandy maelstrom. Lungs bursting, nerveless limbs flailing, the great wave crushed me in its churning maw.

My eyes opened: Black night, icy cold, and infinite silence surrounded me. Far, far above, a beautiful oval of light, like a dancing full moon, hung in the midnight sky. Within it, limned by the light, appearing as if by magic, I saw my father's hand.

"Dad!" I cried out in the darkness, but I heard nothing. My words rose past my outstretched hands in beautiful shimmering orbs. The light above was fading, the moon became a sliver, sickly gray. My eyes closed.

Suddenly his warm, powerful hand closed over mine. He drew me up, the moon banished by the blazing noon, and I was in his arms, eyes stinging, water streaming from nose and mouth, gasping for air. His strong arms supported me as he surged to the shore, my hand now safe in his.

ALL MY YOUNG LIFE I had wanted to be like him.

When I was almost eighteen, senior year in high school, and the time came to look at colleges, I had known immediately that I wanted to follow in his footsteps. "I want to be an engineer. Maybe someday we can work together!" I exclaimed.

He rested a hand on my shoulder. "Maybe," he replied, the shadow of a smile lighting up his bright blue eyes.

I shot off my applications. Despite my less than stellar grades, the Massachusetts Institute of Technology was my first choice. College was going to be a big step, and I wanted it to be a good one. All of February I was on edge, waiting to see if my acceptance letter would arrive. I was shooting for the stars, I knew, but I had the rash confidence of youth.

February became March, and still no letter came from MIT. Many of the other seniors in my class had already heard back from their first and even second choices. I was checking the mail so often, I was starting to wear a groove in the carpet. "My birthday's just a few weeks away. I'm sure to hear back soon," I reasoned.

I was all too right.

The next day was clear and sunny, and by the time I rolled in after school it was spring-warm with that foreshadowing of April that sets your heart singing.

"Mom! I'm home!" I called, letting the door bang closed behind me. I half-heard her reply. The mail was sitting on the hall table. Right on top lay an important-looking envelope, creamy white, embossed, and addressed to me! Heart pounding out of my chest, I stared as though it would magically vanish if I let it out of sight. The return address was Cambridge, Massachusetts. It was from MIT.

Dropping my bag where I stood, I picked up the envelope. It was thin, the smooth paper almost translucent. Sudden misgiving seized me, bringing my heart into my throat. Thin was bad. Just that afternoon I'd overheard one of the other seniors going on about her acceptance letter, how many forms there had been, and how she had spent all afternoon going through the information with her mom.

"Maybe MIT sends those forms in another envelope," I told myself, trying to dispel the yawning pit in my gut. My hands were shaking, an icy chill prickling down my spine. My treacherous heart whispered, "It could be a rejection. . . ."

I stared, desperate to know what was inside, dreading the unspoken possibility. I took a deep breath. Open it, you coward! I thought and tore the flap wide.

Later, I lay in my bed, just staring at the ceiling. My dream, to go away to school, to be like him and study engineering, was in ashes. Still clutching the disastrous news and wallowing in self-pity, I did not even hear him enter my room.

"I wasn't the best student either," he said in a low voice, resting his hand on my shoulder. "I almost didn't graduate high school, and I never thought I'd go to college at all."

Startled, I looked up at him in wide-eyed surprise. How could this be? He was the smartest man I knew, working for one of the best companies in the country!

He paused for a long moment and then continued, "After we were married, and after you and your sister were born, I went to night school. . .working during the day, and studying at night when you were asleep. I wanted to give you all a better life." He paused, looking into the gathering darkness outside my window. "I never gave up until I got my degree. I want you to remember that. Whatever disappointments life may give you, don't give up."

He stood there, silent, for what seemed like an eternity, his hand on my shoulder. Then he gave it a strong squeeze and said, "Mom says dinner's ready. Come on down when you feel like eating."

I nodded, and he left as quietly as he'd appeared. I lay there for a few more minutes, letting his words sink in. It was almost as if I could still feel his fingers, the strength in them, and the passion which drove him to continue. "Okay, Dad," I vowed, "I won't give up."

———— ⟨∾⟩ ————

MY THIRTY-YEAR-OLD HEAD rests on his broad shoulder, arms wrapped around his torso. My tears— the tears of a terrified child—flow from the eyes of a terrified young father. I am completely unmanned. I want to have my fears comforted, my burdens lifted from me. I want to give up.

My wife and I had been living our busy lives, facing the normal challenges that come with raising three small boys. Our second son's cancer diagnosis had shattered us, and the struggle to save his life was consuming every waking hour. Our little family seemed to be in ruins, possibly beyond repair.

I was trying so hard to be strong, to bear up, whatever the burden. Little by little, the immense pressure had grown. That morning we had learned that, despite the most aggressive therapies, my son's treatment had failed. Breaking this news to my parents, especially my dad, had been the last straw. My overtaxed defenses collapsed, and the tears of a broken-hearted child roared out through the breach.

I know I startled him; I startled myself.

As I stood there, shuddering with grief and aching to be comforted, his hands did what mine could not. They held me. I felt the compassion of my father's spirit, more than ever before, flow into me. I was a wounded child, and at the same time a brother, a father, a comrade in arms. My son was facing a deadly disease. I felt powerless to save him. My father understood this great wound in my heart, perhaps better than I did myself.

He allowed me to be broken. He taught me that it was alright to share my pain, and that it did not mean that I'd given up. He held me in his hands, and I was comforted.

MY EYES OPEN. NOTHING has changed. The room is over-bright, artificially cheerful, sterile and expectant. The world, with its day-to-day cares and petty worries, goes on. My heart is broken. My unworthy hand still rests beneath his, unable to allow his release, selfish and weak to the core.

"I cannot let you go," I whisper. "I cannot bear your hands to be mine alone."

The door opens, and my sister, her tresses blond no longer, enters the room. "Mom is back," she says quietly, "with the neurosurgeon. Everyone is here."

She pauses to look down at him, tears streaking her face and reddening her eyes. Unwilling to break the silence, we allow it to gather until she looks up at me, pain written across her face. I remain on my knees, watching his hand and mine rise and fall to the beat of the life support. The door, half ajar, opens wider, and we are joined by my mother and my brother and my other sisters. Everyone is here and it is time.

We array ourselves around him, each of us reaching out with our love and gentle hands. My mother brushes hair back from his broad forehead, caresses his stubbled cheek. The door opens again, and we are joined by the chaplain, a young priest. He performs the rite of Extreme Unction, and he leads us all in the Lord's Prayer.

Peace. From some well of undeserved grace, peace descends upon me.

I know grief, bitter and prolonged, will come. I know also that I will spend the rest of my life missing him, craving both his presence and his approval. What comes as a surprise is the peace.

I see in my mind's eye the last time we spoke. He was sitting alone in the corner of his wide front porch, unseen in the warm darkness of an early-September summer night. From inside I caught the glow of his ever-present cigarette as he took a deep drag. I went out, sitting down opposite him. We had spent the day visiting, and we were preparing to head back home.

"Hey, Dad," I said, "We'll be heading out soon. What're you doing out here?"

He said nothing for a moment, and I followed the glowing tip as it waxed and waned and became a bright spark arcing over the rail into the earth below. I could not see his face, but I could feel his eyes upon me and hear the smile in his voice.

"I'm just enjoying the last days of summer," he said.

That was it. Those words, almost the last I ever heard from him, were the source of my peace—his final and greatest lesson, though I didn't know it then.

I nodded, saying nothing in return, and I sat there across from him, watching his hands as they slipped another cigarette between his lips and cupped the flaring match. The faint glow of the matchhead traced another arc over the rail, as we sat in silence together.

IT IS FINISHED.

His hands rise, and they wipe a tear from my eye. His hands open, and they rest gently on my mother's arm. Later. . . his hands grip and lift, strong enough to carry him home. Even now they guide and they comfort, they play and they shape. They are courageous, and they are broken, and they do not give up.

Don't miss out!

Click the button below and you can sign up to receive emails whenever Michael Lynes publishes a new book. There's no charge and no obligation.

https://books2read.com/r/B-A-VHIF-DNNR

BOOKS 2 READ

Connecting independent readers to independent writers.

Did you love *My Father's Hands*? Then you should read *Angel Stories - Short Story Collection* by Michael Lynes!

Angel Stories - six-story omnibus collection by Michael Lynes. This eBook Bundle features the stories: My Angel Comes, The Tree House, Sunset Beach and a special edition of My Father's Hands.

Read more at Michael Lynes's site.

Also by Michael Lynes

AngelStories Short Story Collection
The Tree House
Spirit
My Angel Comes
Memories to Treasure
Sunset Beach

Christmas Planet Series
Merry EX-mas

Dead Cold Ghost Stories
November Tales

Ghost Stories Collection
A Grave Business
Scary Love
Heart of Gold

SciFi Stories
East of East of Eden
Above All Dust
Life Slice

The Blood Series
It's In The Blood
Destroyer's Blood
First Blood

Standalone

About the Author

MICHAEL LYNES is the Award-Winning Author of The Blood Series. To date, the series has won the New Apply Literary, Indie BRAG Medallion, Readers Favorite for FANTASY and most recently the IAN Book of the Year Selection for Fantasy. The series begins with the novella "It's in the Blood" and continues with Destroyer's Blood. NEW release Book Two - FIRST BLOOD is due out on November 1st 2019.

Book One - "Destroyer's Blood"

Reviewed By Christian Sia for Readers' Favorite Destroyer's Blood: The Adventures of Devcalion: "a gripping fantasy with strong hints of Greek mythology." Meet Devcalion, "Dev," a demigod, son of Prometheus and nephew of Zeus. He has a telepathic sword and a very close friend called Betrayer, "Tray". When we encounter Dev, he and his friend are climbing up Half Dome. An encounter with Hermes changes everything, driving Dev to the last place he wants to be -- Mt. Olympus. Dev and Tray are pulled into a war they never bargained for. With the darkest power in the universe bent on wreaking havoc, do they have any chance of surviving?

Destroyer's Blood has been awarded the Silver Medal for Fantasy in the Readers Favorite Awards for 2019 and has won an Indie B.R.A.G. Medallion for Fantasy. It also won the Solo Medalist in the New Apple Summer eBook Awards for 2019. Book Two - "First Blood" will be released in November of 2019.

His short story collection, "The Fat Man Gets Out of Bed", was chosen solo Medalist Winner in the 2017 New Apple Summer Indie Book awards. His memoir, "There Is A Reaper: Losing a Child to Cancer", was an Indie B.R.A.G. Gold Medallion Honoree , a silver-medal winner Readers' Favorite International Book Awards for Memoir, a medalist in the New Apple Book Awards for Memoir, and a finalist in Independent Author Network Book of the Year award and the Beverly Hills Book Awards.

Most recently Mr. Lynes has been a Contributing Author to the 2019 Ghostly Rites Anthology.

Mr. Lynes was awarded a BSEE degree in Electrical Engineering from Stevens Institute of Technology and currently works as an embedded software engineer. He has four sons, has been married for over thirty years, and currently lives with his wife and youngest son in the beautiful secluded hills of Sussex County, New Jersey.

Read more at <u>Michael Lynes's site</u>.